THIS BOOK IS TOO SMALL

ANNE WOUTERS
thought of this book.
She also drew the pictures.

DUTTON CHILDREN'S BOOKS
NEW YORK

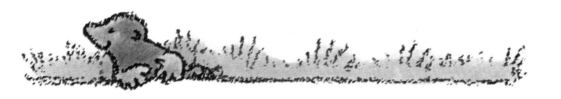

for Christiane

Copyright © 1991 by *l'école des loisirs*, Paris

All rights reserved.

CIP Data is available.

First published in the United States 1992 by
Dutton Children's Books,
a division of Penguin Books USA Inc.
375 Hudson Street, New York, N.Y. 10014

Originally published in Belgium 1991 by
Pastel, 79 Boulevard Louis Schmidt, 1040 Brussels

First American Edition   Printed in Italy
ISBN: 0-525-44881-0   10 9 8 7 6 5 4 3 2 1